Franklin and the Case of the New Friend

Kids Can Press

Franklin always had fun at the park. One day, Franklin and Beaver were playing on the merry-go-round when a piece of paper fluttered off.

"Hey, what's that?" Franklin asked.

They stopped the merry-go-round and picked up the paper.

“It’s a drawing of a skunk family!” said Franklin.
“That’s strange,” said Beaver. “I don’t know any skunk families in Woodland.”
“Me neither,” said Franklin.

"Hey!" said Beaver. "I bet the little skunk in the picture drew this herself."

"Yeah!" said Franklin. "She must have forgotten it."

"Then we should give it back to her," said Beaver. "Maybe she'll want to be our friend!"

"Cool-io!" said Franklin. "But wait — we don't know where she lives."

"It's a real mystery," said Beaver.

"A mystery!" they both shouted. "That sounds like a job for the Super Cluepers!"

Franklin and Beaver raced to the tree house to find the other Super Cluepers. They told them about the new mystery they had to solve.

"We'd better change into our super detective selves!" said Snail.

"I ... am ... Mega Bear," shouted Bear, "the strongest bear of all!"

"I'm Thunder Boy, with a voice like thunder!" Snail boomed.

“You can call me Galaxy Gal,” said Goose, “the girl with the magic wand!”
“And I’m … Green Wonder!” Franklin said.
“I’m Book Whiz!” called Beaver. “Everybody knows that!”
“Kid Gizmo, at your service!” said Fox.
“And I’m Giggler,” said Rabbit, “the funniest guy around!”

The Super Cluepers started their search at the library.
“This book says that skunks often live near forests,” said Book Whiz.
“That’s a great clue!” shouted Thunder Boy.
“Yeah!” everyone cheered.
“I’ll add it to the clue book,” said Book Whiz.

"My, you children are excited today!" said Mrs. Goose, walking over.

"We're going to solve a mystery, and maybe make a new friend!" said Galaxy Gal.

"Well, that sounds fun," said Mrs. Goose with a smile. "Why don't we get your skunk book checked out so you can keep on the clue trail?"

The Super Cluepers left the library and ran to the edge of the forest.

Kid Gizmo peered through his binoculars. "Hey! I think I see something black and white over there!" he said, pointing to a bush nearby.

"It could be a skunk tail!" said Book Whiz. "They're black and white."

Thunder Boy cleared his throat. "Hello!" he boomed. "Little skunk? Are you there?"

There was no answer.

"Let's go find her!" shouted Giggler, running off.

"Yeah!" yelled the rest of the Super Cluepers, racing after him.

"Hello?" Giggler called as he reached the bush. "We brought your drawing back!" He looked behind the bush, but no one was there.

"Hmmm," said Kid Gizmo. "That's strange. I was sure I saw her." He pointed to a red scarf on the ground. "Hey, what's this?" he asked, picking it up with his extendo-arm.

"It looks just like the scarf in the picture!" said Galaxy Gal.

"Another clue!" said Book Whiz. "Time to get out the clue book!"

"Let's all go to my house and figure out what to do next," said Green Wonder.

"Great idea!" said Thunder Boy.

When the Super Cluepers got to Franklin's house, they inspected the scarf.

"Hey, look!" said Giggler. "There's a name sewn onto it. Her name's Skunk!"

"That's another clue for our clue book," said Book Whiz, writing it down.

"Would anyone like a snack?" Mr. Turtle asked, popping into Franklin's room. "I have fresh apple slices!"

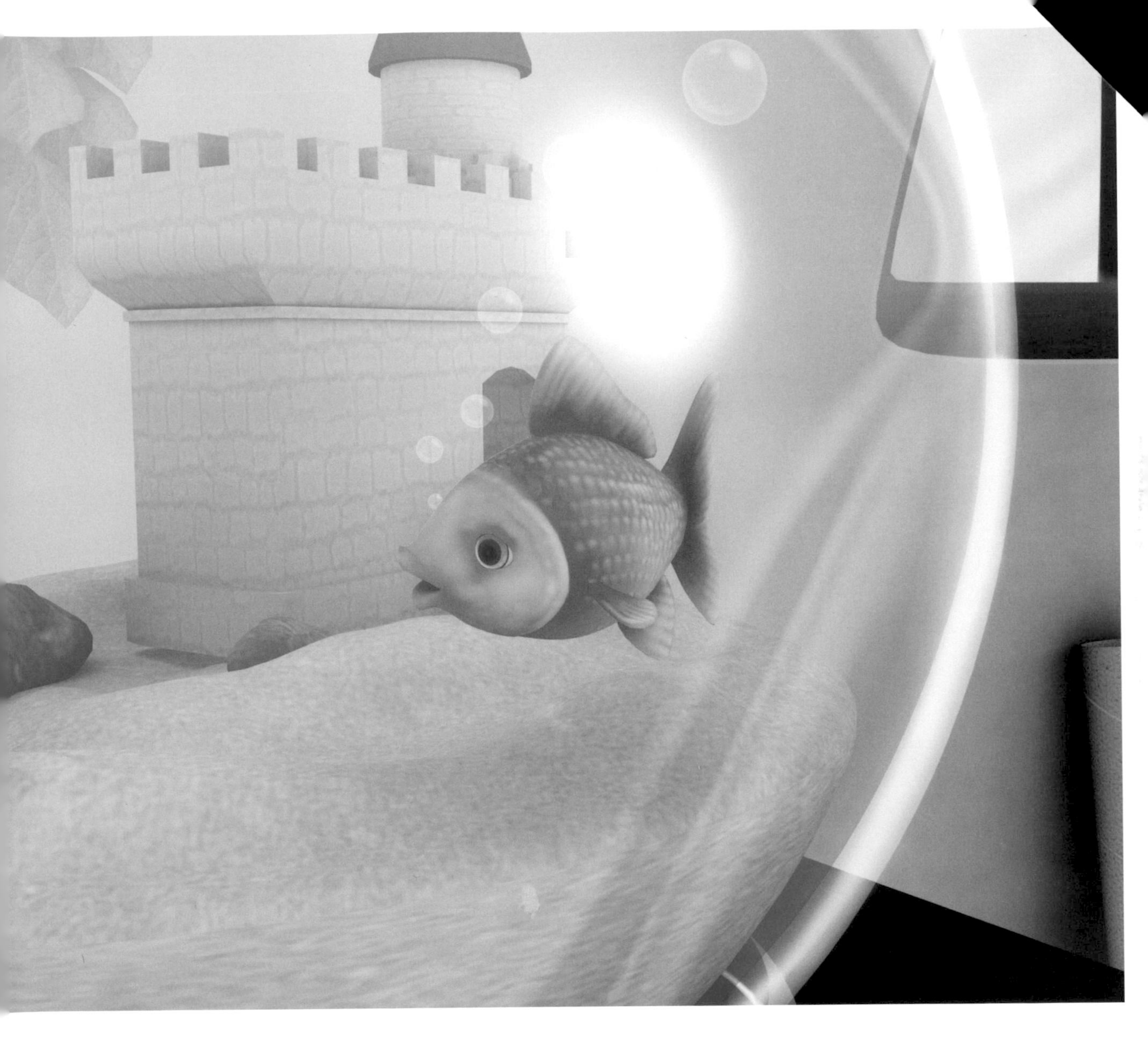

"Yeah!" said the Super Cluepers as they each grabbed an apple slice. "Yum! Thanks, Mr. Turtle!"

"My goodness," said Mr. Turtle. "You kids sure are noisy today." He pointed at Goldie's fishbowl. "Look, you've even managed to scare Goldie!" he said, as he left Franklin's room.

"But why would Goldie be afraid of us?" Mega Bear asked.

"Sometimes Goldie gets shy around lots of people and noise," said Green Wonder. "Hey, that's it!"

"What do you mean?" asked Book Whiz.

“Maybe Skunk didn’t *want* to be found,” said Green Wonder. “Maybe she ran off because she’s shy like Goldie, not because we weren’t friendly enough.”

“You might be right,” said Book Whiz, pointing at a page in the library book. “It says here that skunks are known to be shy!”

“In that case, I think I have a plan,” said Green Wonder.

Later that afternoon, the Super Cluepers headed back to the edge of the forest after making a special gift for Skunk.

"Let's put Skunk's drawing on the ground," said Green Wonder, "where we found her scarf."

"And we'll put her scarf here," said Book Whiz, laying the scarf beside the picture.

"We can put our gift right beside it," said Kid Gizmo, holding up a picture of the Super Cluepers that they had drawn earlier. "That way, when she comes back for her scarf, she'll find her drawing, and ours, too!"

"We're all set," Green Wonder said. "Skunk?" he called softly. "If you can hear us, we put your stuff right here. And we left you a present!"

The Super Cluepers walked away as quietly as they could.

"It's too bad we didn't get to meet our new friend today," said Green Wonder sadly.

"Yeah, but we still did a nice thing," said Galaxy Girl.

"Wait!" a soft voice called from behind the Super Cluepers.

They all turned around. There was Skunk, wearing her scarf and holding up the picture they had drawn for her!

"Whoa!" everyone gasped. "It's *you*!"

"Your picture is really nice," said Skunk shyly. "Thank you!"

"You're welcome," said Green Wonder. "We made it to introduce ourselves. I'm Franklin, but I'm called Green Wonder when I'm solving mysteries — like this one! We were trying to find you to give you your picture back."

"I like mysteries," said Skunk.

The Super Cluepers smiled and introduced themselves one by one.

"My name's Skunk," said Skunk. "I've seen you playing all around Woodland, but I've been too shy to come say hello. You're always so loud and excited when you're together. That's why I left you that picture."

"You left that picture for us?" Green Wonder said.

"Yes," said Skunk. "I wanted you to know who I was, so I left it where I knew you would find it."

"We're really glad you came out to meet us," said Thunder Boy.
"You can come play with us anytime you want," said Green Wonder.
"I'd like that," said Skunk.
"You can even join the Super Cluepers!" said Book Whiz. "We still have one mystery to solve. Now that we've met, does that mean we're friends?"
"Definitely!" said Skunk, smiling.